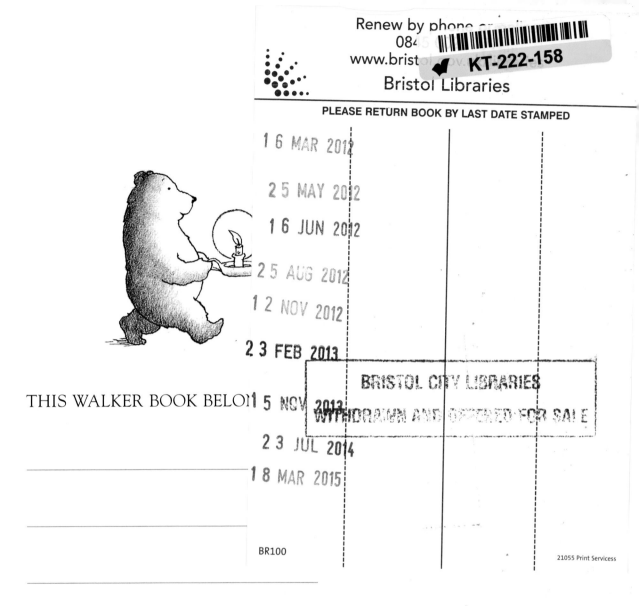

THIS WALKER BOOK BELONGS TO

First published 2006 by Walker Books Ltd,
87 Vauxhall Walk, London SE11 5HJ

This edition published 2007

10 9 8 7 6 5 4 3 2 1

This book has been typeset in Goudy

Printed in Singapore

British Library Cataloguing in Publication Data: a catalogue record for this book is available from the British Library

ISBN 978-1-4063-0533-3

www.walkerbooks.co.uk

MIA'S STORY
MICHAEL FOREMAN

WALKER BOOKS
AND SUBSIDIARIES
LONDON · BOSTON · SYDNEY · AUCKLAND

I will never forget the day I met Mia. My bus
had broken down and I found myself in her village.
We made friends at once and I want
to tell you about her. This is Mia's story.

Mia's village was called Campamento San Francisco and was somewhere between the big city and the snowy mountains. It was not much of a place, but for Mia it was her home and her world.

There are no pretty gardens or trees.
There isn't a proper road, just a muddy track.

Mia's papa and his truck

He goes to the city every day to sell scrap.

It used to be farmland but the city grew bigger and bigger and now they can only harvest what the city throws away.

This is Mia's house.

Mia's mama

The houses are made from odds and ends and bits of rubbish, whatever the people can find.

Nia's school

The children love playing football.

These are the ovens where the villagers bake their bread.

They are very clever at fixing things they find on the dumps.

Sometimes Papa comes home happy
with money in his pockets
and sometimes he comes home sad
with none.

Mia runs to meet her papa
every evening.

Mia's father dreamed of one day being
able to build a house of bricks.

One evening in early autumn Mia's father came home with a strange grin on his face. He unzipped his jacket and there was a beautiful puppy! Papa had found him all alone in the city.

Mia kissed her new puppy on the nose. She
decided to call him Poco because he was so small.

Mia showed the puppy to everyone and soon he was part of her life.

Poco likes his new family.

Poco licks Mia's face then Mama's face and then Papa's face.

Mia shows Poco to Sancho.

Hello Sancho!

Poco follows Mia everywhere – even to school.

He is very good and waits outside until the end of lessons.

But it was a hard winter and one day Poco disappeared. Mia searched the village, then she climbed onto Sancho and set off to look through the dumps.

A pack of dogs went that way. He could have been with them.

Have you seen my little dog?

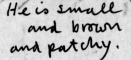

He is small and brown and patchy.

Come on, Sancho. We'll
find him.

Poco! Poco!

As she searched she got further and further from home.

Until eventually she found herself
high up in the mountains, far higher
than she had been before. From
up there she could look down
on the dark cloud
that always filled
the valley.

The air above the cloud was so clean it took Mia's breath away. She was dazzled by the whiteness all around. She jumped down from Sancho and grabbed the snow, tasting it and rolling over and over in the whole white world of it.

Sancho watched her and then he too rolled over and kicked his old legs in the air. Then Mia lay on her back, arms and legs outstretched in the snow. The sky had never been so blue and so near.

They called and searched for Poco until night began to fall and the first stars appeared. Mia was exhausted but she knew that Sancho would take her safely home.

They set off slowly until suddenly he stopped and snuffled at the ground. Mia looked around. Instead of snow they were now surrounded by flowers. Mia carefully gathered a clump, roots and all. She knew that whatever happened they would remind her of how she looked for Poco and found this place in the stars.

The next day, Mia planted the flowers.

She pots some in tin cans.

She tends them
and waters them
everyday.

The flowers grow tall and strong and they spread in the summer.

In the autumn the wind blows seeds all over the village.

The flowers spread quickly. By the following spring they had spread all over the village and the dumps were covered with flowers as white as the mountain snow.

Although she enjoyed looking after the flowers, Mia never forgot Poco and called for him every day.

One morning when her father was leaving for the city with a load of scrap to sell, Mia said she wanted to go with him to try and sell her flowers. She pointed to rows of white flowers in tin cans. Her father laughed and agreed to give it a try.

Mia put her flowers on the steps of the cathedral
and Papa laid out his scrap nearby.

The main square is busy with traders.

Rain or shine.

There are always lots of musicians.

What a beautiful baby!

Not sold much today?

Soon Mia had so many customers, Papa
had to give up his scrap business to help
sell flowers. People asked, "Where
do these flowers come from?"
And Mia said, "They come
from the stars."

From that day on Mia and Papa sold flowers and shared his dream of building a house of bricks. And whenever a pack of dogs came running by, Mia thought of Poco.

Until one day one of the dogs stopped running
and came to smell the flowers. He licked
Mia's face and lay down among them.

I was travelling from Santiago, Chile, into the Andes mountains and

came upon what appeared to be a wasteland – a landscape of waste from the city.

But a man who lived there, Manuel, showed me it was the opposite of a wasteland.

For Manuel and his fellow villagers, the waste was a crop to be harvested,

recycled and made useful once more.

for Manuel and his family.
may you have a house of bricks
one day.

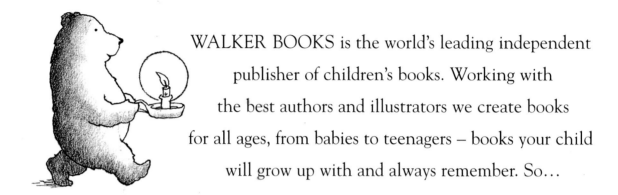

WALKER BOOKS is the world's leading independent publisher of children's books. Working with the best authors and illustrators we create books for all ages, from babies to teenagers – books your child will grow up with and always remember. So…

FOR THE BEST CHILDREN'S BOOKS, LOOK FOR THE BEAR